London 1930

She walked down on an obscure alley on a cold October night; with her white dress, curly hair and big brown eyes; you can hear the men in the pubs nearby; She was running to take a taxi on her journey home; apparently the date that she attended wasn't that pleasant as she expected; she rushed in a taxi to take her far away as he could drive from the smelly alley that she was walking in. She arrived home, and put herself to bed, staring at the moon; "What should I do? I need to run away from all of these problems". She took her coat and rush with her little suitcase down the stairs. She took a taxi to the Kings Cross Train Station and she jumped in to the first train that will take her far away as she wanted.

She arrived after 2 hours and 45 minutes to a little town near by the sea, with a lovely view of a lighthouse and cold stone water in front of her; She dropt her suitcase in her hotel room, and run down to the sea shore; Was such a cold peaceful sunrise, that you could see the sun and moon going up and down in the same time; She walked with no stress down to the shore hopping her soul finds peace and love again in her heart; She walked and walked with no sense of time;

October is not such a nice period in London, and the rain started to poor over her curly hair; She was so happy and dancing in the rain that she didn't mind of the tiny drops that wet her white face; In her happiness she notice a figure getting out of the cold water and running to the shore; He was the most pleasant figure that she ever did see in her life; Big blue eyes, curly eyelashes, blond curly hair, fit allure.

She watched him for a couple of minutes but for her was an eternity; There eyes connected and he was looking at her very simple like he didn't care of her presence staring at him naked; "I'm guessing your familiar with the cold water?"

"I'm guessing you can mind your own business"; "I'm guessing you don't have any manners to talk to a lady like that";

"I'm sorry for my manners, miss...?"

"Cecilia...I'm Cecilia"; she murmured

"Darren!! Nice to meet you miss Cecilia"

"So I'm guessing the cold water serves you good, I suppose?"

"You're guessing too much Miss Cecilia. How about you? The rain serves you good I suppose too?"

"Very funny, but I'm afraid yes, it does."

"I never see around these areas, what brings you around the shore?"

"Actually I'm kind of lost. I was wondering around too much apparently..."

"Is getting kind a cold, my house is just near the coast, if you want you can come and warm up a bit."

"OH. Thank you, but I don't walk in strangers home just like that, perhaps you misunderstood me"

"As you wish!"

He left running in her eyes like mad, while she was left behind in a cold rain with nobody to guide her back home; A hard knock at the door!!!;

"Hey! Come on in. Darren murmured.

"I only came because is a very bad wheatear outside"

"I didn't ask for regrets miss Cecilia, you can make yourself confortable and I'll bring you some towels and some tea." She was looking at him under her hair; examine every inch of his body and face. She didn't realized what she was doing in a stranger that she just met; she wasn't like that, what she was thinking?

"Here you go fresh towels and a warm cup of tea."

"Thank you, I don't want to disturb you too much from your work. I can see you have a lot of papers and an old writing machine. Are you a writer?"

"I was! Not anymore."

"Why that?"

"Is personal miss Cecillia."

"Im sorry,I didn't mean to disturb you,il be on my way!"

"NO! I didn't mean to say that, I just don't talk about my personal life,that's all.Im sorry if I was a bit mean,im not used to visitors anymore."

"Ok...I understand.Can I ask you why you leave her alone?"

"After my mom passed away I came her,I promise her will take care of the shore house,it was her all life."`

"Ohh..i understand.Im sorry about your mother,really...I know how is to be alone,I have lost my father in the war and my mom left us when I was young."

"Us?"

"Yes.Us.Me and my little brother .He is 14 this year.I miss him so much.I will see him at the end of this year."

"Im happy for you that you have a brother,im alone.So if your dry you can spend the night on the bed and il take the sofa,miss Cecillia.

"That is very kind of you,but I must be on my way..."she murmured.

"Have you looked outside?f you go out know,you wont make it until the shore,is a very bad weather.

"Ok il stay.Thank you again Darran for everything."

She crushed on his bed,and fall asleep straight away...He was looking at her from the corner of his sofa,just watching her how beautiful she was.

"Wake up!Cecillia!!! Wake up!!"

"Oh god! What happened?!"Cecillia asked.

"You had a nightmare,you were ok now,calm down."

"Im very sorry,I didn't want to wake you up..."

"Is ok,I wasn't asleep.I was watching you."

"Watching me?"she murmured.

"Im sorry,go back to sleep."

She grab his hand and in the next minute,her lips touched his,and her tong rush inside his mouth like she wanted to discover him and feel him all over her body.His hands grab her waist and push her to his body like he posed her.Her white milky skin touch his body as he tooked her breast in his arms.He trow her in the bed and fill her with passion and love all night long.

"What time is it?"Cecillia asked.

"Is 10 am miss Cecillia,I made you breakfast."Darran looked at her with a smile in his face.

"Ohh god!What happened last night?Im so sorry I need to leave now!"

Darran hold her arm and looked at her,like he never wanted to let her leave never from his side.

"Cecillia...,stay!"

"Im sorry Darran,I was upset and I was lonely and I don t know I don't want to hurt you...im very sorry."

"Miss Cecillia...stay!Please."

"Im sorry Darran!"

She run out on the wet sand,and never looked back.She run until she arrived at her room,crushed down and start crying until her face was covered with wet long tears.She didn't want this to happened,but she was happy in a strange way,she feelt something for him,happiness and joy ,and she didn't feel that for a long time.Next day,she packed her stuff and went back to the shore house,back to him.With her suitcase in her arm she knocked at his door with tears in her eyes.

"Yes?"

"Cecillia??"I didn't expect you here,after last night."

"Im sorry Darran,I don t want you to think nothing bad about me,what happened last night was a big and huge mistake,I came to tell you im leaving and I want to thank you for last night,for giving me a place to stay."

"Your leaving?Where?"

"Back to London,to my home."

"Cecillia,miss Cecillia...don't go..."

"Im sorry,you don't understand!We have nothing,I don't know you,I don't know who are you.Im leaving,goodbye."

Before she finished her words,he grab her in his arms and clouse the door behind them,he put his arm to her mouth and wissper to her ear:"I want you,I want you to stay with me,I want you Ceccilia,I need you."

"I need you,im in love with you,I want you,you don't understand,you are the girl that I been writing my books about,the grl of my dreams,I cant let you go."

"What is wrong with you?Let my go Darran.We have nothing,let my go ."

He went to her lips and tell her:"If you didn't feel nothing why you make love to me last night like crazy?Why you let my feel you all over my body,why you let me make your passions and desires come true?"Hmm?"

"Darran....ohhhhh"

He kissed her like crazy,grab her mouth and put her next to his.It was passion and hate and desire and love,she feelt that and she love it.

"Darran...make love to me,make me yours one more time!!!"

He took her in his powerfull arms and put her over the table,he took her breast in his arms and kissed them like crazy.She was moaning of desire and screaming his name.He loved her once more,but this time was different,it wasn't soft and with love,it was hard and with passion like he will never see her again.

"Darran,I want you too,that s why im going because we cant be togheder,I have important things to do and it is impossible....please let my go.

"Il make love to you every second if that s is the only metod that I can keep you next to me.Il make love to you and every way and in every corner,il rape your body in so many ways Cecillia....I need you..."

"Ohhh Darran,I need you so badly in my life,I need you in my heart...but is impossible.Trust me,it cannot be."

"Tell me your address in London,il come to you.Tommorow,il pack all and come to you.Il fiind someone to take care of the house till im gone."

"Darran,is impossible!"

"WHY?Tell my why? Because im just a failed writer?Idont have money to offer you?I don t have houses in London.Why Cecillia?Why?"

"Im married!...."

"What?he smiled like crazy.That is not true."

"Im married,im sorry Darran."

“You used me,you just wanted to feel another man on top of you...I was just a puppet...no?Anser me!!!!!!!!”

“Please don’t scream....Darran!No!You aren’t a puppet,I like it I wanted,I need you,I ... i.....i have feeling for you.....but is impossible...”

“Get out of my house!NOW!”

“Darran....”

“OUT!”

He cryed watch her run on the shore in her emty foot..I was the first time in his life that he feel in love and the first time that he had his heart turn to pieces...The feeling was mutual....He hated hiself for letting that happened...

Cecillia pop in the first train to London,as she was looking on the window,her tears were falling on her white cheeks...She loved him,but she couldn’t hurt him more than she already did.

She arrived at this big mansion whit whit gates and lion head on the door.

“Miss Cecillia,your back!So fast?”

“Hy Carmin,is my husband home?”

“Yes, he is in the back as usual.”

“Thank you.”

“I was expecting you maybe next week, Cece.”

“Well I surprised you, no Bill?”

“You did”. Said a grumpy old man playing golf in his back yard.

“I want the divorce...Bill.”

"Ohh... Cece, you still don't learn, I will never give you the divorce, is the part of our bargain, you forgot?"

"I will never love you,you make me sick."

"Tonight make yourself beautiful,I want to spend it with you."

"I hate you,if my father would be alive...

"But he is not!And he told me to marry you and you know that!So your my wife,and I want you tonight!Is that clear?"

"You make me sick Bill..."

"Listen you little whore,I let you everytime to run away and do your things,and I never punished you,so you don't want me to don't keep my part of the deal and little Tommy has to suffer no?"

'Don't you speak about my little brother, you old shit!"

"I see you need a punissment,get up now!"

He grab her by her arm and pushed her against the wall, took her dress up and fill her with hate.She was thinking of Darran and her eyes start crying and screaming for help.

"See...Cece,how difficult is this,to make love to me everytime I desire.Your my wife,and you need to start getting use to it,or is gone be bad for both of you."

She run up and start crying over her soft big white pillows.She wanted so many times to end her life,but her little brother was her life!!She needed to accept her bargain.After her dad was killed in the war,all of her fortune was taken by the military and she was on the streets with little Tommy,until she fiind out of her fathers friend.The bargain was to marry him,and he will provide them all the money that they need.So it was impossible for her to leave the old man...

"Miss Ceciilia...Senior Bill wants you to come downstairs.Someone is looking for you."

"Ok, il be down in 5 minutes."

She went down,and when she arrived her eyes pop into tears,her little brother was there.

"Ceceeeeee!!!"

"Tommy,come here!"

It was the most happy moment in her life,feeling her little brother next to her and alive.

"How big you areeee!!!I missed you!"But you suppose to be here in two mounths,why now?"

"Bill came and get me today in the morning from school,because he said we gone go in a great vacantion,I cant wait"

"Ok,go up in my room and unpack,il come later."

"Why didn't tell me about Tommy?"

"Because I wanted to be a surprise,Cece that s why."

"Im his sister,you don't make him surprises,you are nothing to him!"

"Hmmm,well I think im all for him,I pay for his school,I pay for his home,I pay for all no?"

“I don’t want you near him.Do you understand me?”

“Listen,go and pack, tomorrow we are leaving.”

“WHAT?Where?Im not going!”

“Listen Cecillia,you are getting on my last nerv,I said go and pack!Tommorow morning we are going in a vacantion,like a family.”

“Im not going!”

“Hmmm is the last time that I say,go and pack or I need to use force,Cecillia, and you don’t want little Tommy to see that,wont we?”

“I will get you one day,for this Bill..”

“Oh and mister Carmin,please try to find a replacement for you until you leave for your holidays, try to be someone nice, I don’t to fire him from the first day?

“Yes Sir Bill of course, right away.”

The next morning they left in vacation, with little Tommy so happy and Cecilia so sad...You could see her tears rushing down her cheeks, as she was departing from home...

After 3 weeks...

Ohh. .Sir Bill welcome back. How was your vacation Sir? Did you enjoy?

Good morning Carmin! Yes it was amazing. Little Tommy here, enjoyed the most of course.

How about you, miss Cecillia? It was fun?

Superb. Thank you, Carmin!

Don't you worry Carmin, she will get in to her shoes, as soon as I will have a chat with her.

I will go upstairs, please, if I'm excused.

Of course, miss Cecillia. Answers Carmin.

Well...Carmin? Did you find someone to replace you?

Yes Sir. Of course. I found a lad that is quite good. I think you should keep him here. To help me with the house.

Come on. I want to meet him.

Of course Sir. He is in the garden.

Hello there my boy! I'm the guy who pays you. How is work until now?

Well, good morning Sir Bill. I'm very well, thank you. The job is perfect, I really need it the money.

I'm very glad then my boy. If you need something please do tell.

Indeed. Thank you, Sir.

The master is very kind to people who help him, so don't blow this one up, kid.

I won't, Carmin. Thank you.

Cecillia???? Where are you???

I'm here Tommy, I'm coming.

Come on let's play in the garden.

Is to sunny Tommy, we need shade, air and water.

Come on you big baby!

I'm the baby? Look who is talking? Come here you!

In that moment Cecillia's eyes took contact with Darran's ....Cecillia couldn't realize is she was dreaming or it was true. The man that took her heart away, was in front of her, smiling.

Tommy go inside and play. Now Tommy!!!

What the hell are you doing here?

This is how you introduce yourself miss Cecillia? The big rich girl? With the old guy you are married? To bad of you...Such a beautiful innocent girl...

Shut up! You're not in the right position to judge me. You kick me out of your house in the middle of a hurricane.

Yes...After I found out that you are married!??!

Please leave! How did you find me?

Ohhh...Please! Do you really imagine that I was chasing you? Please Cecillia, you are not that precious to track down.

I'm gone slap you! And I will tell Bill that you harassed me and he will fire you straight away.

Listen you crazy women. Carmin is my uncle, he knew that I needed some extra cash so he asked me if I want this job, to help him while he is away. I didn't know that the rich old champ is your husband and most certainly I didn't know that you are the wife. So is better that you shut up and try to act like we don't know each other.

Ok I'm sorry. I didn't knew. Of course Il pretend I don't know you... Are you crazy?

Scared of big Bill to find out?

Are you blackmailing me?

I would never do that, is just funny. You should see your face.

Bill is coming. Act normal.

Well hi there my little flower? Feeling better?

Yes, Bill. Thank you. Much better.

Good. Then you will join my for dinner tonight. We have a guest.

I' m so sorry, but I think I prefer to rest. I don't feel confortable with new people around me.

Cecillia! You will join my for dinner, and that's it. At 7 in the lobby. Dress nice please.

Bill...

Don't make me take Mr. Whip outside in front of our guests...Love you sweatheart.

Please tell me that Mr. Whip is a dog.

No...It is not a dog. See you later Darran. I need to get ready for my guests.

Darran started to figure it out what was happening to Cecillia, but he couldn't understand why she was leaving with such a monster.

It was 7 pm, and the dinner was served in the big lobby of the mansion. The guest arrived along with his wife, and Mr. Bill was waiting for his own. Cecillia came 10 minutes past 7 o'clock. She was dressed like a big royalty with purple flowers around her head.

Well, my lovely guest, this is my beautiful wife, Cecillia.

Wow! She is so young and beautiful! Said the wife of the ugly little fellow that was Mr. Bill guest.

Indeed she is! Thank you. My love please have a seat next to me.

Cecillia was full of anger and hate when she was looking at Bill. In her mind was just her little brother and how to escape this evil plan that never ended.

The dinner was quite. After a few hours the guest left and everybody was preparing to go to sleep.

Il be excuse!

Where are you going?

In my room Bill. I want to rest.

Darran just came into the room to help the house cleaning lady with the plates. Cecillia looked him and in his eyes ,and you could see that she was begging for help. Darran couldn't do nothing to help her, because he didn't know the real truth, why she is still here and not running like hell to the door.

Tonight you are sleeping with me, my sweet wife.

NO! Bill please... Don't force me.

I said that you are sleeping with me, so you better go upstairs and I will come in a bit to keep you company.

Cecillia was waiting for him in his bedroom. She was scared of what he can do to her.

Why every time you need to make my life so hard? Why Cecillia? Why? You enjoy? You like driving me crazy??!!

Please Bill... Why are you keeping me here? You know I'm never gone love you. I hate you. I only thank you for taking me and Tommy. But you take us with half of my father' fortune. You can complain. I told you I don't want nothing. Is all yours.

I just want my brother and my memories that you have with my father and we are gone. I promise. You will never see us again.

Hmmm... You promise?

Yes! I promise Bill. Please...

You stupid! Ever crossed your mind that I would actually leave you to go? You will never go. I took you to make you my wife and sleep with you whenever I want, when I want and where I want. I took care of that boy like it was my own. He didn't miss a penny. I send him to the best schools, I give him everything and this is how you thank me? Come on Cecillia get up! You are so weak... You would never be like your dad, you and that little boy. You are week and I fill pity for you. You should never complain...it is just sex Cecillia! I'm not hurting you.. I didn't ask for nothing just to keep me company. See what you have done? Know I need to keep you locked until the bruises go away.

No... please Bill... don't keep me locked. Il tell everybody that I fall down. They will believe me. Please. Il do whatever you want but please...

Ok...get out of my room.

Spring 1918

What happened to your face?

Nothing. I just fall down and hit myself. So stupid no?

You could fool maybe Tommy, Cecillia but not me. That maniac hit you?

Darran! Stop asking questions that will never get answers. Just let it go. I did.

Are you stupid or what? Why are you doing this to yourself? Take Tommy and go.

Darran, listen is not simple at all. I need to stay for my brother, to keep him safe.

Keep him safe from whom?

From the world outside. I want him to have all of the joy and beautiful things and the world. The ones I had before I had to get married.

Cecillia listen to me, please...

Darran! Thank you for showing me again the feeling of love and passion, but you will never understand. I need to stay with Bill, he helps Tommy and he will give him a future.

Yes Cecillia, but I think different, when Tommy will grow up and he will find out that you sacrifice for him like that, you think that he will be happy? He will not. He will be accusing himself that you did all of this stuff and you weren't happy.

Darran just leave it like it is. Please.

Ok Cecillia but trust me you will remember my words after years...

After years maybe we will meet in different life, Darran...

Cecillia??

Yes Bill, I am in the garden.

Cecillia I need to go for two days out of town with work. You will be ok?

Yes! Don't worry Bill, I will be fine. Take care of you.

Ok. See you soon. If you need something send after me.

Sure. Drive safe Bill. Take care.

Are you mad???

Let go of me, Darran! You are hurting me!

Seriously? Take care? To that maniac? Who is heating you like a animal?

You don't understand... Are you crazy or what? He is the reason that I'm leaving this life. He is the reason that Tommy has a normal life and has all that he will ever want. I told you...you don't understand and you will never, Darran. I love you with all my heart, but it will never be anything between us. Just let it go.

Tommy come down for dinner!

Coming Cecillia.

And wash your hands, please!

Ok...ok...

Miss Cecillia, it is a letter for you...

Thank, please leave it on the desk I will take it after we finish diner.

A....i think you may want to read it now....

What it so important? Probably just some taxes to be paid. Bill will handle those when he is coming back tomorrow.

Miss Cecillia...please...

From whom is it, god??

It is from your father....

What?? Is this some kind a sick joke?

No...your lawyer came today and delivered personally and he said that he is moving out of London. He say to tell you farewell and to be safe.

Give me that letter. Tommy stay here and eat your diner!

But I want to read what dad says!

Your dad is dead Tom! This letter probably is a joke.

But...

Tom! Stay here!

Cecillia?

Darran this is not a good time, please.

What happened ?

Cecillia rush in the library and shut the door. She didn't know what to do with the letter. She wanted to throw it in to the fire, but she will have to leave with the guilt forever that she never knew what was written in that letter.

She open it... The letter was from her father just 1 day before he died. Cecillia started crying and her tears fall on her cheeks like rain in the ocean.

My dear Cecillia,

I'm very sorry I have to leave you and Tommy alone in this world, after I promise your mother that I will take care of you. I wish I could see you and my son happy and all grown up. I wrote this letter even if I'm not supposed to do it, as part of my arrangement with Bill and a couple of lawyers, but I want you to know what is gone happened for the future. Bill will take care of you and your brother until Tommy will make 21 years old. He will provide you with money, food, home and all the best things that you gone need. Don't worry about nothing. He will have access to my money after my dead, and he will spend it only on you and your brother. You know Bill, so please try to make him happy and to behave all the time. He is the only one that I can give him my money and know that he will give all of it to you. I don't trust your uncle or your aunt, as you know they were always after my goods.

I know is gone be hard for you to understand this, but you need to know that all of it is for you and your brother. You need to marry Bill so you can have full access of my money and his money also. You will have to live with him until Tom makes 21 years. At his 21 years, one of the lawyers, will come and broke the contract that is been made. Bill is not allowed to refuse it, as he can go to jail be marring a minor. I know it sounds very awful, but it was the only option that I had to give you my money safe. Don't tell Tom this now, let him know when he is 21, so he can process and fully understand.

I love you Cecillia, I will always do. You are so much like your mother and that is why you keep me alive so much time. Take care of Tom and also of you. I hope after all of this, you can find your happiness and peace.

Love,

DAD

Cecillia now understand all of it. She was in peace all ready. She knew she will be free in a couple of years. And she knew she will have everything for Tommy and they go far away from Bill and London.

Cecillia? May I come in?

Yes! Yes! Said Cecillia laughing.

A... are you ok?

Yes Darran! It is the happiest day in my life. Now I know I didn't suffer in vain. All of it will come to an end sooner or later.

Well...I'm happy for you, but I don't understand nothing.

Oh my little dear boy, you don't have to. Maybe after a couple of years we can run away, move I don't know in Venice and have kids. Ha ha ha...

Cecillia are you ok? Why we need to wait? Why we can run now?

We can't! Well I can't. You can run if you want, but first make love to me Darran. Make love right here on this floor...now!

Darran hold her body close to his, and touch her so gently, like the wind touches the field flowers. He made love to her all over the floor, over and over again until the sun run away and the moon was knocking at the window.

That was amazing Darran. We need to this again sometimes.

What do you mean sometimes? We are not...

Darran! Please! I told you. I can't be with you the way I want. I have feelings for you and I do love you. You make me alive again. But that's it. Nothing else. I'm a married woman.

Whit a maniac!!!! You call him your husband?

Darran. Shht. I told you, you can't understand.

Then make me Cecillia! Make me understand. Because I'm going crazy here.

Darran, I told you I love you and that is enough for me. I can't promise you things that I know I can't hold them. Like I told you, maybe in a few years we gone meet somewhere if god wants and we can be happy. But for now, this is the only thing that I can provide you. Nothing else, I can't divorce Bill, at least not now.

I will never understand you, even if is for the money, you can manage yourself to go away with Tommy and me. We can be a family.

Darran...stop! Please. I know what I'm doing now, I just needed a bit of sense in my life, and I have it now.

Among the years...

Darran never understood Cecillia and her mind, but he carry along with her for on and on and on... He loved her. He really believed that he can help her to leave Bill and go with him. He tried even to force her one night to run away with him. Cecillia was so in love she was so close to do it, until she remember her father's letter. She couldn't run, why now? Why should she run away when she will have her freedom in 3 years . But things got difficult...Darran wanted a baby, as the years went by... all the love that Darran had for Cecillia begin fading away.

He was looking at her how she pretended to be happy with Bill. How the years went by and Cecillia still stay next by her husband. Tommy was a grow man now, going to the best colleges and taking piano lessons.

Darran?!

Yes...Cecillia. What happened?

Darran.. Is something wrong? Why are you avoiding me? What happened with you?

With me? Are you serious right now? You really want to know what is wrong with me? Ok. I will tell you. How about that is been almost 7 years and we are hiding like high school kids!! God damn it!!!

Shht! Keep your voice down.

Why? So your 60 years husband don't hear me? The one that you sleep next to for so many years, every night? And I'm sleeping alone like an idiot and thinking when can we be happy?

Tell me Cecillia! That the years pass by and I'm still here because of you.

Because of me? I never asked you to stay here trapped. I told you to go. And I will follow someday.

Someday?? Ha... someday... When? Tell me when?

I don't know. Why can you be different?

Different? Are you even listening right now? To do what, stay like an idiot another 7,10, 20 years to wait until the old man dies?

2 years. That's it. Just give me 2 more years and I'm yours.

I can't do it anymore Cecillia. You need to decide yourself, is gone be me or him. Or not, is gone be the money and luxury that I can't never offer you, or me.

Don't do this Darran. Don't do something you will regret.

I will regret. I know I will. But at least I can be free. At least I can find someone and start fresh again. Have a family. A family I always wanted to. I'm sorry Cecillia, but you ran out of time.

Cecillia??

Yes Tommy...

What happened with you and Darran?

Nothing...nothing Tommy. Don't worry.

Cecillia, I don't want to see you sad. Why you don't divorce Bill? Be happy.

You will understand when the time is gone be Tommy. Now don't you worry with your big sister problems. You need to study for your exams, mister.

Yeah, I was doing that but Bill told me something and I wanted to tell you.

Tell me, what that old scam want.

He sold the house. And he got a really good deal. We are moving to America, sis!

Cecillia was heartbroken. She new that was the end of her and Darran.

Sis! Hey! Where are you going?

Bill! Why you didn't tell me?

Ah! Tommy told you. We are moving to America in 1 week. So start packing.

What...? In one week?

Yes. America Cecillia! Don't worry the divorce is legal in any country. I'm an old man anyway. So I'm not gone be here forever.

I don't know what to say...Why you didn't tell me?

Well me and Tom knew from like a month ago. He was with the idea. Smart lad. Nothing like his sister, by the way.

I don't care how your calling me...2 more years and I'm done with this.

Yes, but trust me Cecillia, you will miss me. I'm not worry about you, I'm worry about your brother. You need to take care of him. And by falling in love with some peasant I'm not quite sure that you will do that.

My brother means the world to me. I will sacrifice everybody and everything for him. So don't you worry about Tommy.

Hey guys? Dinner is ready.

Thank you Tommy my boy, we are coming now.

You go. I need to go something.

Ok. But don't be late, I'm hungry.

Cecillia? Are you in here? You missed dinner, are you ok? Sis?

Bill! Come quick! Bill! Sis, sis! What is wrong with you? Wake up!

What happened Thomas? Oh my god! Cecillia?

Call an ambulance Thomas now! Cecillia what did you do to yourself?

Cecillia? My love?

Your love? What the hell you think you are you peasant? In my house you are telling to my wife love?

She loves me with all her heart. She will never love you Bill, you need to understand!

I kept you in my house, because of your uncle, you better thank him boy, because if it wasn't for him, you be in jail.

Try me!

Don't push it Darran, don't push it. Anyway in 1 week we are moving in America so say goodbye to her now. Because this, all of this, was nothing! Your nothing to her, just someone younger to play around with.

It's a lie! 1 week? No...

Bye-bye Darran.

Miss Cecillia? Are with us?

What happened? My head is spinning.

Well, you are pregnant! Congratulations.

I'm what? Sorry? I ca....no it's impossible!

I'm a doctor miss Cecillia, I'm pretty sure I know how to do my job.

You don't understand, I can't be. With who?

With your husband...He is here. Excuse me.

Cecillia...Are you ok? How do you feel?

Make the abortion Bill, I will do it tonight. I don't want your child. It is impossible. You can accept this. It is illegal Bill and you know that.

Cecillia, in the contract doesn't say nothing about that. I'm sorry. I will not kill a innocent child because of you. It is my child. My only child. I'm sorry.

What? Are you crazy? First of all how do you know it is even yours? Is not yours Bill, is not. Is my child and I will do what I want with it.

Listen to me, that is a human inside you is not a it! And is mine! Darran didn't touch you since long time ago, I could feel it in your reactions, so don't lie to me because I'm an old man Cecillia, I know things better then you. Good night, take a good rest. Tomorrow we are going home.

No...Bill.. please. No...

Tommy? Tom?

Yes Darran, what is it?

Please how is your sister? I'm going crazy here.

Darran why are you still here? You are going in 3 days...

What? 3 days? Your dad told me a week yesterday.

Yes, well my sister is pregnant and she is sick so she needs to rest. So we are leaving early.

Pregnant?!? She is pregnant?

Listen, is not you ok? She is pregnant with Bill. And he is not my dad. Cecillia never told you, but when I'm gone be 21 she and Bill will get divorce and me and her will gone get all of my dad's money. She needs to stay married with him, that was part of the contract. Now she is pregnant, and it was a mistake, but Bill doesn't want to leave her like this, with child. So she will keep the baby. And she will leave you, because she will not lose all of it for you, Darran. I'm sorry, I'm really sorry, I like you but my sister can be with you. I don't understand why see didn't tell you from the begging, so you don't make so many plans with someone that has already plans with someone else.

But she will be divorce in what? 2 years?

Did you listen to me? Is not your baby! Get over it Darran. Leave. Find someone else, be happy, you deserved it. You are a good guy.

Kid, I love your sister more than my life. If Bill kills me, I don't care. I need to see her. She would never do this to me.

She is in the garden...

Are you feeling better?

What do you want Darran? Why are you still here?

Are you joking? I'm the happiest man alive. I can't believe, it is a miracle.

What are you talking about?

Tommy told me, I'm gone be a father.

What? You? Your not gone be nothing Darran.

What are you talking about Cecillia?

You want to hear this from me, ok then let me tell you. I slept will Bill when you didn't want me, I was lonely and I needed affection. I'm a women Darran, I'm not of steel. He is my husband and I made love to him. I got pregnant very simple and I'm having a baby. We are leaving to America in 3 days, and there I will give birth. After, I'm gone get divorce, give to Bill the child to take care of him or her until he gone pass way. Then I'm gone take it and take care of him because I'm his mother. Tommy will grow up a handsome man and he will finish his university in New York, and me? I will go to Bill grave every Sunday and cry, cry so bad that he left me alone, and then I will think of you. I will think that I loved you with all my heart but we couldn't be happy, and then I will move on. Maybe I will send you a letter and maybe you will answer me.

So this is it? Me and you? You are giving up us so easy? Like nothing ever matter? How could you sleep with him? How could you lay there next to him after making love, when I was alone 2 floors downstairs thinking how the hell to run away from this place? Did you ever loved me? Or you love him? You know what I think, that you always love him Cecillia. You don't know, but you love him, you cant live without him.

Shut up! You are disgusting.

You are Cecillia. I'm so sick of myself loving you. I love you. I love you with all of my heart. I was hoping that child to be mine, to be a girl beautiful as you, to love her like I loved you. Why Cecillia? Why did you do this to me? Why?

I loved you, but you need to understand if I leave all of it now, I lose my brother, I lose my child, I lose my money, my house, everything. For nothing?

Nothing? That is what you call me now? Nothing?

Darran, please go. You would never understand what is happening in my heart. I'm happy that I met you and I will never forget you. But my life is complicated and it will always be.

I hope your father is proud of you. I'm pretty sure that this is not what he wanted you to become.

Darran? Darran?

Cecillia? Let's go. It's time to pack everything. Bill told me to take you upstairs.

Why Tommy? Why?

Cecillia, listen you need to put yourself together for us. Come on. Let's go.

Bill, I'm so sorry for everything. I should new that you will never lie to me and take care of us. I'm so sorry...

It's ok love, don't worry. You did what every stupid young girl should do, I always knew that you come back to your senses. Come on let's go.

Guys, please can you take care of the rest of the house and furniture. If mister Bob comes to move, please tell him to contact me and I will explain why I have to leave.

Of course Sir, don't worry about nothing.

Come on Cecillia up you go. Come on Tommy you to.

The carriage start moving, leaving everything behind...

Cecillia?! Cecillia!!! Don't leave me, don't leave us. Please. Cecillia!!!

As the carriage was leaving the yard, Cecillia didn't have the power to look back and see Darran like this. She wanted to keep him in her mind like he was. A strong man who loved her with all his heart.

Cecillia don't do this, don't go. Cecillia...

Darran, it's over! Come on I will take you upstairs.

Leave me alone! Go away! You took her from me. And him. And everybody. All of you. Let me be...

The hours pass by, and as Cecillia was far far away from London, Darran was still there waiting for her. He couldn't imagine that all that they had for so many years, went by, like the wind.

Mate? It's over. I need to close the mansion, tomorrow the new owner is moving in. Nobody is coming back. You need to go.

Tommy, did you talk with your sister?

They are in the way to America, 2 more days I think with the ship. Cecillia is happy and safe.

How do you know that she is happy? She told you? Or Bill told you?

Doesn't matter how told me, she is better then here.

Well, I'm sure she is not. Because nobody asked her how she feels, if she is happy, if she needs something. It was only about you Tommy. You and him.

Me?

Yes, Tommy. You. Because if wasn't you, she could run away with me and be happy. She could be a woman, not a slave.

Listen Darran, I'm gone be honest with you. If Cecillia wanted to run away with you, I'm sure she would. You know why? Because if she left me with Bill, I don't think he will just throw me in the street. He care about me and he loved me. So I'm guessing that if she stayed with him for so many years, is because she wanted and maybe she loved him in her way. So be a man and get over it. It was a dream, a dream that you knew someday you gone wake up and it's over. I'm going...I hope you will find your true fate Darran, stay safe.

Bye Tommy. Send Cecillia my love when you see her.

I will. I promise.

Take care, kid.

Darran left from London back to his homeland. He knew that all of it wasn't a dream, it was love. The true meaning of love. He would never forget her, as she would never forget him.

In one early raining morning, he open the newspaper and the daily news was:

'Luxury Cruise Ship sank last night in the middle of the Atlantic Ocean'...
No survivors. A lot of important people lost their lives on the ship. Unfortunately no passengers survive the impact with the powerful storm.

The news stroke Darran's heart like an arrow. He would only imagine Cecillia's face when she was happy next to him, when they make love for hours and hours. He couldn't believe that the love of his life is dead. He couldn't breathe no more, his eyes were full of tears and his hands wrapped on the newspaper.

After all of this, apparently love is not the only thing in life that keeps us together.

London 1930

She walked down on an obscure alley on a cold October night; with her white dress, curly hair and big brown eyes; you can hear the men in the pubs nearby; She was running to take a taxi on her journey home; apparently the date that she attended wasn't that pleasant as she expected; she rushed in a taxi to take her far away as he could drive from the smelly alley that she was walking in. She arrived home, and put herself to bed, staring at the moon; "What should I do? I need to run away from all of these problems". She took her coat and rush with her little suitcase down the stairs. She took a taxi to the Kings Cross Train Station and she jumped in to the first train that will take her far away as she wanted.

She arrived after 2 hours and 45 minutes to a little town near by the sea, with a lovely view of a lighthouse and cold stone water in front of her; She dropt her suitcase in her hotel room, and run down to the sea shore; Was such a cold peaceful sunrise, that you could see the sun and moon going up and down in the same time; She walked with no stress down to the shore hopping her soul finds peace and love again in her heart; She walked and walked with no sense of time;

October is not such a nice period in London, and the rain started to poor over her curly hair; She was so happy and dancing in the rain that she didn't mind of the tiny drops that wet her white face; In her happiness she notice a figure getting out of the cold water and running to the shore; He was the most pleasant figure that she ever did see in her life; Big blue eyes, curly eyelashes, blond curly hair, fit allure.

She watched him for a couple of minutes but for her was an eternity; There eyes connected and he was looking at her very simple like he didn't care of her presence staring at him naked; "I'm guessing your familiar with the cold water?"

“I’m guessing you can mind your own business”; “I’m guessing you don’t have any manners to talk to a lady like that”;

“I’m sorry for my manners, miss…?”

“Cecilia…I’m Cecilia”; she murmured

“Darren!! Nice to meet you miss Cecilia”

“So I’m guessing the cold water serves you good, I suppose?”

“You’re guessing too much Miss Cecilia. How about you? The rain serves you good I suppose too?”

“Very funny, but I’m afraid yes, it does.”

“I never see around these areas, what brings you around the shore?”

“Actually I’m kind of lost. I was wondering around too much apparently…”

“Is getting kind a cold, my house is just near the coast, if you want you can come and warm up a bit.”

“OH. Thank you, but I don’t walk in strangers home just like that, perhaps you misunderstood me”

“As you wish!”

He left running in her eyes like mad, while she was left behind in a cold rain with nobody to guide her back home; A hard knock at the door!!!;

“Hey! Come on in. Darren murmured.

“I only came because is a very bad wheatear outside”

“I didn’t ask for regrets miss Cecilia, you can make yourself confortable and I’ll bring you some towels and some tea.” She was looking at him under her hair; examine every inch of his body and face. She didn’t realized what she was doing in a stranger that she just met; she wasn’t like that, what she was thinking?

“Here you go fresh towels and a warm cup of tea.”

“Thank you, I don’t want to disturb you too much from your work. I can see you have a lot of papers and an old writing machine. Are you a writer?”

“I was! Not anymore.”

“Why that?”

“Is personal miss Cecillia.”

“Im sorry,I didn’t mean to disturb you,il be on my way!”

“NO! I didn’t mean to say that, I just don’t talk about my personal life,that’s all.Im sorry if I was a bit mean,im not used to visitors anymore.”

“Ok...I understand.Can I ask you why you leave her alone?”

“After my mom passed away I came her,I promise her will take care of the shore house,it was her all life.”`

“Ohh..i understand.Im sorry about your mother,really...I know how is to be alone,I have lost my father in the war and my mom left us when I was young.”

“Us?”

“Yes.Us.Me and my little brother .He is 14 this year.I miss him so much.I will see him at the end of this year.”

“Im happy for you that you have a brother,im alone.So if your dry you can spend the night on the bed and il take the sofa,miss Cecillia.

“That is very kind of you,but I must be on my way...”she murmured.

“Have you looked outside?f you go out know,you wont make it until the shore,is a very bad weather.

“Ok il stay.Thank you again Darran for everything.”

She crushed on his bed,and fall asleep straight away...He was looking at her from the corner of his sofa,just watching her how beautiful she was.

“Wake up!Cecillia!!! Wake up!!”

“Oh god! What happened?!”Cecillia asked.

“You had a nightmare,you were ok now,calm down.”

“Im very sorry,I didn’t want to wake you up...”

“Is ok,I wasn’t asleep.I was watching you.”

“Watching me?”she murmured.

“Im sorry,go back to sleep.”

She grab his hand and in the next minute,her lips touched his,and her tong rush inside his mouth like she wanted to discover him and feel him all over her body.His hands grab her waist and push her to his body like he posed her.Her white milky skin touch his body as he tooked her breast in his arms.He trow her in the bed and fill her with passion and love all night long.

“What time is it?”Cecillia asked.

“Is 10 am miss Cecillia,I made you breakfast.”Darran looked at her with a smile in his face.

“Ohh god!What happened last night?Im so sorry I need to leave now!”

Darran hold her arm and looked at her,like he never wanted to let her leave never from his side.

“Cecillia...,stay!”

“Im sorry Darran,I was upset and I was lonely and I don t know I don’t want to hurt you...im very sorry.”

"Miss Cecillia...stay!Please."

"Im sorry Darran!"

She run out on the wet sand,and never looked back.She run until she arrived at her room,crushed down and start crying until her face was covered with wet long tears.She didn't want this to happened,but she was happy in a strange way,she feelt something for him,happiness and joy ,and she didn't feel that for a long time.Next day,she packed her stuff and went back to the shore house,back to him.With her suitcase in her arm she knocked at his door with tears in her eyes.

"Yes?"

"Cecillia??"I didn't expect you here,after last night."

"Im sorry Darran,I don t want you to think nothing bad about me,what happened last night was a big and huge mistake,I came to tell you im leaving and I want to thank you for last night,for giving me a place to stay."

"Your leaving?Where?"

"Back to London,to my home."

"Cecillia,miss Cecillia...don't go..."

"Im sorry,you don't understand!We have nothing,I don't know you,I don't know who are you.Im leaving,goodbye."

Before she finished her words,he grab her in his arms and clouse the door behind them,he put his arm to her mouth and wissper to her ear:"I want you,I want you to stay with me,I want you Ceccilia,I need you."

"I need you,im in love with you,I want you,you don't understand,you are the girl that I been writing my books about,the grl of my dreams,I cant let you go."

"What is wrong with you?Let my go Darran.We have nothing,let my go ."

He went to her lips and tell her:“If you didn’t feel nothing why you make love to me last night like crazy?Why you let my feel you all over my body,why you let me make your passions and desires come true?”Hmm?”

“Darran....ohhhhh”

He kissed her like crazy,grab her mouth and put her next to his.It was passion and hate and desire and love,she feelt that and she love it.

“Darran...make love to me,make me yours one more time!!!”

He took her in his powerfull arms and put her over the table,he took her breast in his arms and kissed them like crazy.She was moaning of desire and screaming his name.He loved her once more,but this time was different,it wasn’t soft and with love,it was hard and with passion like he will never see her again.

“Darran,I want you too,that s why im going because we cant be togheder,I have important things to do and it is impossible....please let my go.

“Il make love to you every second if that s is the only metod that I can keep you next to me.Il make love to you and every way and in every corner,il rape your body in so many ways Cecillia....I need you...”

“Ohhh Darran,I need you so badly in my life,I need you in my heart...but is impossible.Trust me,it cannot be.”

“Tell me your address in London,il come to you.Tommorow,il pack all and come to you.Il fiind someone to take care of the house till im gone.”

“Darran,is impossible!”

“WHY?Tell my why? Because im just a failed writer?Idont have money to offer you?I don t have houses in London.Why Cecillia?Why?”

“Im married!....”

“What?he smiled like crazy.That is not true.”

“Im married,im sorry Darran.”

“You used me,you just wanted to feel another man on top of you...I was just a puppet...no?Anser me!!!!!!!!”

“Please don’t scream....Darran!No!You aren’t a puppet,I like it I wanted,I need you,I ... i.....i have feeling for you.....but is impossible...”

“Get out of my house!NOW!”

“Darran....”

“OUT!”

He cryed watch her run on the shore in her emty foot..I was the first time in his life that he feel in love and the first time that he had his heart turn to pieces...The feeling was mutual....He hated hiself for letting that happened...

Cecillia pop in the first train to London,as she was looking on the window,her tears were falling on her white cheeks...She loved him,but she couldn’t hurt him more than she already did.

She arrived at this big mansion whit whit gates and lion head on the door.

“Miss Cecillia,your back!So fast?”

“Hy Carmin,is my husband home?”

“Yes, he is in the back as usual.”

“Thank you.”

“I was expecting you maybe next week, Cece.”

“Well I surprised you, no Bill?”

“You did”. Said a grumpy old man playing golf in his back yard.

“I want the divorce...Bill.”

"Ohh… Cece, you still don't learn, I will never give you the divorce, is the part of our bargain, you forgot?"

"I will never love you,you make me sick."

"Tonight make yourself beautiful,I want to spend it with you."

"I hate you,if my father would be alive…

"But he is not!And he told me to marry you and you know that!So your my wife,and I want you tonight!Is that clear?"

"You make me sick Bill…"

"Listen you little whore,I let you everytime to run away and do your things,and I never punished you,so you don't want me to don't keep my part of the deal and little Tommy has to suffer no?"

'Don't you speak about my little brother, you old shit!"

"I see you need a punissment,get up now!"

He grab her by her arm and pushed her against the wall, took her dress up and fill her with hate.She was thinking of Darran and her eyes start crying and screaming for help.

"See…Cece,how difficult is this,to make love to me everytime I desire.Your my wife,and you need to start getting use to it,or is gone be bad for both of you."

She run up and start crying over her soft big white pillows.She wanted so many times to end her life,but her little brother was her life!!She needed to accept her bargain.After her dad was killed in the war,all of her fortune was taken by the military and she was on the streets with little Tommy,until she fiind out of her fathers friend.The bargain was to marry him,and he will provide them all the money that they need.So it was impossible for her to leave the old man...

"Miss Ceciilia...Senior Bill wants you to come downstairs.Someone is looking for you."

"Ok, il be down in 5 minutes."

She went down,and when she arrived her eyes pop into tears,her little brother was there.

"Ceceeeeee!!!"

"Tommy,come here!"

It was the most happy moment in her life,feeling her little brother next to her and alive.

"How big you areeee!!!I missed you!"But you suppose to be here in two mounths,why now?"

"Bill came and get me today in the morning from school,because he said we gone go in a great vacantion,I cant wait"

"Ok,go up in my room and unpack,il come later."

"Why didn't tell me about Tommy?"

"Because I wanted to be a surprise,Cece that s why."

"Im his sister,you don't make him surprises,you are nothing to him!"

"Hmmm,well I think im all for him,I pay for his school,I pay for his home,I pay for all no?"

“I don’t want you near him.Do you understand me?”

“Listen,go and pack, tomorrow we are leaving.”

“WHAT?Where?Im not going!”

“Listen Cecillia,you are getting on my last nerv,I said go and pack!Tommorow morning we are going in a vacantion,like a family.”

“Im not going!”

“Hmmm is the last time that I say,go and pack or I need to use force,Cecillia, and you don’t want little Tommy to see that,wont we?”

“I will get you one day,for this Bill..”

“Oh and mister Carmin,please try to find a replacement for you until you leave for your holidays, try to be someone nice, I don’t to fire him from the first day?

“Yes Sir Bill of course, right away.”

The next morning they left in vacation, with little Tommy so happy and Cecilia so sad...You could see her tears rushing down her cheeks, as she was departing from home...

After 3 weeks...

Ohh. .Sir Bill welcome back. How was your vacation Sir? Did you enjoy?

Good morning Carmin! Yes it was amazing. Little Tommy here, enjoyed the most of course.

How about you, miss Cecillia? It was fun?

Superb. Thank you, Carmin!

Don't you worry Carmin, she will get in to her shoes, as soon as I will have a chat with her.

I will go upstairs, please, if I'm excused.

Of course, miss Cecillia. Answers Carmin.

Well...Carmin? Did you find someone to replace you?

Yes Sir. Of course. I found a lad that is quite good. I think you should keep him here. To help me with the house.

Come on. I want to meet him.

Of course Sir. He is in the garden.

Hello there my boy! I'm the guy who pays you. How is work until now?

Well, good morning Sir Bill. I'm very well, thank you. The job is perfect, I really need it the money.

I'm very glad then my boy. If you need something please do tell.

Indeed. Thank you, Sir.

The master is very kind to people who help him, so don't blow this one up, kid.

I won't, Carmin. Thank you.

Cecillia???? Where are you???

I'm here Tommy, I'm coming.

Come on let's play in the garden.

Is to sunny Tommy, we need shade, air and water.

Come on you big baby!

I'm the baby? Look who is talking? Come here you!

In that moment Cecillia's eyes took contact with Darran's ....Cecillia couldn't realize is she was dreaming or it was true. The man that took her heart away, was in front of her, smiling.

Tommy go inside and play. Now Tommy!!!

What the hell are you doing here?

This is how you introduce yourself miss Cecillia? The big rich girl? With the old guy you are married? To bad of you...Such a beautiful innocent girl...

Shut up! You're not in the right position to judge me. You kick me out of your house in the middle of a hurricane.

Yes...After I found out that you are married!??!

Please leave! How did you find me?

Ohhh...Please! Do you really imagine that I was chasing you? Please Cecillia, you are not that precious to track down.

I'm gone slap you! And I will tell Bill that you harassed me and he will fire you straight away.

Listen you crazy women. Carmin is my uncle, he knew that I needed some extra cash so he asked me if I want this job, to help him while he is away. I didn't know that the rich old champ is your husband and most certainly I didn't know that you are the wife. So is better that you shut up and try to act like we don't know each other.

Ok I'm sorry. I didn't knew. Of course Il pretend I don't know you... Are you crazy?

Scared of big Bill to find out?

Are you blackmailing me?

I would never do that, is just funny. You should see your face.

Bill is coming. Act normal.

Well hi there my little flower? Feeling better?

Yes, Bill. Thank you. Much better.

Good. Then you will join my for dinner tonight. We have a guest.

I' m so sorry, but I think I prefer to rest. I don't feel confortable with new people around me.

Cecillia! You will join my for dinner, and that's it. At 7 in the lobby. Dress nice please.

Bill...

Don't make me take Mr. Whip outside in front of our guests...Love you sweatheart.

Please tell me that Mr. Whip is a dog.

No...It is not a dog. See you later Darran. I need to get ready for my guests.

Darran started to figure it out what was happening to Cecillia, but he couldn't understand why she was leaving with such a monster.

It was 7 pm, and the dinner was served in the big lobby of the mansion. The guest arrived along with his wife, and Mr. Bill was waiting for his own. Cecillia came 10 minutes past 7 o'clock. She was dressed like a big royalty with purple flowers around her head.

Well, my lovely guest, this is my beautiful wife, Cecillia.

Wow! She is so young and beautiful! Said the wife of the ugly little fellow that was Mr. Bill guest.

Indeed she is! Thank you. My love please have a seat next to me.

Cecillia was full of anger and hate when she was looking at Bill. In her mind was just her little brother and how to escape this evil plan that never ended.

The dinner was quite. After a few hours the guest left and everybody was preparing to go to sleep.

Il be excuse!

Where are you going?

In my room Bill. I want to rest.

Darran just came into the room to help the house cleaning lady with the plates. Cecillia looked him and in his eyes ,and you could see that she was begging for help. Darran couldn't do nothing to help her, because he didn't know the real truth, why she is still here and not running like hell to the door.

Tonight you are sleeping with me, my sweet wife.

NO! Bill please... Don't force me.

I said that you are sleeping with me, so you better go upstairs and I will come in a bit to keep you company.

Cecillia was waiting for him in his bedroom. She was scared of what he can do to her.

Why every time you need to make my life so hard? Why Cecillia? Why? You enjoy? You like driving me crazy??!!

Please Bill... Why are you keeping me here? You know I'm never gone love you. I hate you. I only thank you for taking me and Tommy. But you take us with half of my father' fortune. You can complain. I told you I don't want nothing. Is all yours.

I just want my brother and my memories that you have with my father and we are gone. I promise. You will never see us again.

Hmmm... You promise?

Yes! I promise Bill. Please...

You stupid! Ever crossed your mind that I would actually leave you to go? You will never go. I took you to make you my wife and sleep with you whenever I want, when I want and where I want. I took care of that boy like it was my own. He didn't miss a penny. I send him to the best schools, I give him everything and this is how you thank me? Come on Cecillia get up! You are so weak... You would never be like your dad, you and that little boy. You are week and I fill pity for you. You should never complain...it is just sex Cecillia! I'm not hurting you.. I didn't ask for nothing just to keep me company. See what you have done? Know I need to keep you locked until the bruises go away.

No... please Bill... don't keep me locked. Il tell everybody that I fall down. They will believe me. Please. Il do whatever you want but please...

Ok...get out of my room.

Spring 1918

What happened to your face?

Nothing. I just fall down and hit myself. So stupid no?

You could fool maybe Tommy, Cecillia but not me. That maniac hit you?

Darran! Stop asking questions that will never get answers. Just let it go. I did.

Are you stupid or what? Why are you doing this to yourself? Take Tommy and go.

Darran, listen is not simple at all. I need to stay for my brother, to keep him safe.

Keep him safe from whom?

From the world outside. I want him to have all of the joy and beautiful things and the world. The ones I had before I had to get married.

Cecillia listen to me, please...

Darran! Thank you for showing me again the feeling of love and passion, but you will never understand. I need to stay with Bill, he helps Tommy and he will give him a future.

Yes Cecillia, but I think different, when Tommy will grow up and he will find out that you sacrifice for him like that, you think that he will be happy? He will not. He will be accusing himself that you did all of this stuff and you weren't happy.

Darran just leave it like it is. Please.

Ok Cecillia but trust me you will remember my words after years...

After years maybe we will meet in different life, Darran...

Cecillia??

Yes Bill, I am in the garden.

Cecillia I need to go for two days out of town with work. You will be ok?

Yes! Don't worry Bill, I will be fine. Take care of you.

Ok. See you soon. If you need something send after me.

Sure. Drive safe Bill. Take care.

Are you mad???

Let go of me, Darran! You are hurting me!

Seriously? Take care? To that maniac? Who is heating you like a animal?

You don't understand... Are you crazy or what? He is the reason that I'm leaving this life. He is the reason that Tommy has a normal life and has all that he will ever want. I told you...you don't understand and you will never, Darran. I love you with all my heart, but it will never be anything between us. Just let it go.

Tommy come down for dinner!

Coming Cecillia.

And wash your hands, please!

Ok...ok...

Miss Cecillia, it is a letter for you...

Thank, please leave it on the desk I will take it after we finish diner.

A....i think you may want to read it now....

What it so important? Probably just some taxes to be paid. Bill will handle those when he is coming back tomorrow.

Miss Cecillia...please...

From whom is it, god??

It is from your father....

What?? Is this some kind a sick joke?

No...your lawyer came today and delivered personally and he said that he is moving out of London. He say to tell you farewell and to be safe.

Give me that letter. Tommy stay here and eat your diner!

But I want to read what dad says!

Your dad is dead Tom! This letter probably is a joke.

But...

Tom! Stay here!

Cecillia?

Darran this is not a good time, please.

What happened ?

Cecillia rush in the library and shut the door. She didn't know what to do with the letter. She wanted to throw it in to the fire, but she will have to leave with the guilt forever that she never knew what was written in that letter.

She open it... The letter was from her father just 1 day before he died. Cecillia started crying and her tears fall on her cheeks like rain in the ocean.

My dear Cecillia,

I'm very sorry I have to leave you and Tommy alone in this world, after I promise your mother that I will take care of you. I wish I could see you and my son happy and all grown up. I wrote this letter even if I'm not supposed to do it, as part of my arrangement with Bill and a couple of lawyers, but I want you to know what is gone happened for the future. Bill will take care of you and your brother until Tommy will make 21 years old. He will provide you with money, food, home and all the best things that you gone need. Don't worry about nothing. He will have access to my money after my dead, and he will spend it only on you and your brother. You know Bill, so please try to make him happy and to behave all the time. He is the only one that I can give him my money and know that he will give all of it to you. I don't trust your uncle or your aunt, as you know they were always after my goods.

I know is gone be hard for you to understand this, but you need to know that all of it is for you and your brother. You need to marry Bill so you can have full access of my money and his money also. You will have to live with him until Tom makes 21 years. At his 21 years, one of the lawyers, will come and broke the contract that is been made. Bill is not allowed to refuse it, as he can go to jail be marring a minor. I know it sounds very awful, but it was the only option that I had to give you my money safe. Don't tell Tom this now, let him know when he is 21, so he can process and fully understand.

I love you Cecillia, I will always do. You are so much like your mother and that is why you keep me alive so much time. Take care of Tom and also of you. I hope after all of this, you can find your happiness and peace.

Love,

DAD

Cecillia now understand all of it. She was in peace all ready. She knew she will be free in a couple of years. And she knew she will have everything for Tommy and they go far away from Bill and London.

Cecillia? May I come in?

Yes! Yes! Said Cecillia laughing.

A... are you ok?

Yes Darran! It is the happiest day in my life. Now I know I didn't suffer in vain. All of it will come to an end sooner or later.

Well...I'm happy for you, but I don't understand nothing.

Oh my little dear boy, you don't have to. Maybe after a couple of years we can run away, move I don't know in Venice and have kids. Ha ha ha...

Cecillia are you ok? Why we need to wait? Why we can run now?

We can't! Well I can't. You can run if you want, but first make love to me Darran. Make love right here on this floor...now!

Darran hold her body close to his, and touch her so gently, like the wind touches the field flowers. He made love to her all over the floor, over and over again until the sun run away and the moon was knocking at the window.

That was amazing Darran. We need to this again sometimes.

What do you mean sometimes? We are not...

Darran! Please! I told you. I can't be with you the way I want. I have feelings for you and I do love you. You make me alive again. But that's it. Nothing else. I'm a married woman.

Whit a maniac!!!! You call him your husband?

Darran. Shht. I told you, you can't understand.

Then make me Cecillia! Make me understand. Because I'm going crazy here.

Darran, I told you I love you and that is enough for me. I can't promise you things that I know I can't hold them. Like I told you, maybe in a few years we gone meet somewhere if god wants and we can be happy. But for now, this is the only thing that I can provide you. Nothing else, I can't divorce Bill, at least not now.

I will never understand you, even if is for the money, you can manage yourself to go away with Tommy and me. We can be a family.

Darran...stop! Please. I know what I'm doing now, I just needed a bit of sense in my life, and I have it now.

Among the years...

Darran never understood Cecillia and her mind, but he carry along with her for on and on and on... He loved her. He really believed that he can help her to leave Bill and go with him. He tried even to force her one night to run away with him. Cecillia was so in love she was so close to do it, until she remember her father's letter. She couldn't run, why now? Why should she run away when she will have her freedom in 3 years . But things got difficult...Darran wanted a baby, as the years went by... all the love that Darran had for Cecillia begin fading away.

He was looking at her how she pretended to be happy with Bill. How the years went by and Cecillia still stay next by her husband. Tommy was a grow man now, going to the best colleges and taking piano lessons.

Darran?!

Yes...Cecillia. What happened?

Darran.. Is something wrong? Why are you avoiding me? What happened with you?

With me? Are you serious right now? You really want to know what is wrong with me? Ok. I will tell you. How about that is been almost 7 years and we are hiding like high school kids!! God damn it!!!

Shht! Keep your voice down.

Why? So your 60 years husband don't hear me? The one that you sleep next to for so many years, every night? And I'm sleeping alone like an idiot and thinking when can we be happy?

Tell me Cecillia! That the years pass by and I'm still here because of you.

Because of me? I never asked you to stay here trapped. I told you to go. And I will follow someday.

Someday?? Ha... someday... When? Tell me when?

I don't know. Why can you be different?

Different? Are you even listening right now? To do what, stay like an idiot another 7,10, 20 years to wait until the old man dies?

2 years. That's it. Just give me 2 more years and I'm yours.

I can't do it anymore Cecillia. You need to decide yourself, is gone be me or him. Or not, is gone be the money and luxury that I can't never offer you, or me.

Don't do this Darran. Don't do something you will regret.

I will regret. I know I will. But at least I can be free. At least I can find someone and start fresh again. Have a family. A family I always wanted to. I'm sorry Cecillia, but you ran out of time.

Cecillia??

Yes Tommy...

What happened with you and Darran?

Nothing...nothing Tommy. Don't worry.

Cecillia, I don't want to see you sad. Why you don't divorce Bill? Be happy.

You will understand when the time is gone be Tommy. Now don't you worry with your big sister problems. You need to study for your exams, mister.

Yeah, I was doing that but Bill told me something and I wanted to tell you.

Tell me, what that old scam want.

He sold the house. And he got a really good deal. We are moving to America, sis!

Cecillia was heartbroken. She new that was the end of her and Darran.

Sis! Hey! Where are you going?

Bill! Why you didn't tell me?

Ah! Tommy told you. We are moving to America in 1 week. So start packing.

What...? In one week?

Yes. America Cecillia! Don't worry the divorce is legal in any country. I'm an old man anyway. So I'm not gone be here forever.

I don't know what to say...Why you didn't tell me?

Well me and Tom knew from like a month ago. He was with the idea. Smart lad. Nothing like his sister, by the way.

I don't care how your calling me...2 more years and I'm done with this.

Yes, but trust me Cecillia, you will miss me. I'm not worry about you, I'm worry about your brother. You need to take care of him. And by falling in love with some peasant I'm not quite sure that you will do that.

My brother means the world to me. I will sacrifice everybody and everything for him. So don't you worry about Tommy.

Hey guys? Dinner is ready.

Thank you Tommy my boy, we are coming now.

You go. I need to go something.

Ok. But don't be late, I'm hungry.

Cecillia? Are you in here? You missed dinner, are you ok? Sis?

Bill! Come quick! Bill! Sis, sis! What is wrong with you? Wake up!

What happened Thomas? Oh my god! Cecillia?

Call an ambulance Thomas now! Cecillia what did you do to yourself?

Cecillia? My love?

Your love? What the hell you think you are you peasant? In my house you are telling to my wife love?

She loves me with all her heart. She will never love you Bill, you need to understand!

I kept you in my house, because of your uncle, you better thank him boy, because if it wasn't for him, you be in jail.

Try me!

Don't push it Darran, don't push it. Anyway in 1 week we are moving in America so say goodbye to her now. Because this, all of this, was nothing! Your nothing to her, just someone younger to play around with.

It's a lie! 1 week? No...

Bye-bye Darran.

Miss Cecillia? Are with us?

What happened? My head is spinning.

Well, you are pregnant! Congratulations.

I'm what? Sorry? I ca....no it's impossible!

I'm a doctor miss Cecillia, I'm pretty sure I know how to do my job.

You don't understand, I can't be. With who?

With your husband...He is here. Excuse me.

Cecillia...Are you ok? How do you feel?

Make the abortion Bill, I will do it tonight. I don't want your child. It is impossible. You can accept this. It is illegal Bill and you know that.

Cecillia, in the contract doesn't say nothing about that. I'm sorry. I will not kill a innocent child because of you. It is my child. My only child. I'm sorry.

What? Are you crazy? First of all how do you know it is even yours? Is not yours Bill, is not. Is my child and I will do what I want with it.

Listen to me, that is a human inside you is not a it! And is mine! Darran didn't touch you since long time ago, I could feel it in your reactions, so don't lie to me because I'm an old man Cecillia, I know things better then you. Good night, take a good rest. Tomorrow we are going home.

No...Bill.. please. No...

Tommy? Tom?

Yes Darran, what is it?

Please how is your sister? I'm going crazy here.

Darran why are you still here? You are going in 3 days...

What? 3 days? Your dad told me a week yesterday.

Yes, well my sister is pregnant and she is sick so she needs to rest. So we are leaving early.

Pregnant?!? She is pregnant?

Listen, is not you ok? She is pregnant with Bill. And he is not my dad. Cecillia never told you, but when I'm gone be 21 she and Bill will get divorce and me and her will gone get all of my dad's money. She needs to stay married with him, that was part of the contract. Now she is pregnant, and it was a mistake, but Bill doesn't want to leave her like this, with child. So she will keep the baby. And she will leave you, because she will not lose all of it for you, Darran. I'm sorry, I'm really sorry, I like you but my sister can be with you. I don't understand why see didn't tell you from the begging, so you don't make so many plans with someone that has already plans with someone else.

But she will be divorce in what? 2 years?

Did you listen to me? Is not your baby! Get over it Darran. Leave. Find someone else, be happy, you deserved it. You are a good guy.

Kid, I love your sister more than my life. If Bill kills me, I don't care. I need to see her. She would never do this to me.

She is in the garden...

Are you feeling better?

What do you want Darran? Why are you still here?

Are you joking? I'm the happiest man alive. I can't believe, it is a miracle.

What are you talking about?

Tommy told me, I'm gone be a father.

What? You? Your not gone be nothing Darran.

What are you talking about Cecillia?

You want to hear this from me, ok then let me tell you. I slept will Bill when you didn't want me, I was lonely and I needed affection. I'm a women Darran, I'm not of steel. He is my husband and I made love to him. I got pregnant very simple and I'm having a baby. We are leaving to America in 3 days, and there I will give birth. After, I'm gone get divorce, give to Bill the child to take care of him or her until he gone pass way. Then I'm gone take it and take care of him because I'm his mother. Tommy will grow up a handsome man and he will finish his university in New York, and me? I will go to Bill grave every Sunday and cry, cry so bad that he left me alone, and then I will think of you. I will think that I loved you with all my heart but we couldn't be happy, and then I will move on. Maybe I will send you a letter and maybe you will answer me.

So this is it? Me and you? You are giving up us so easy? Like nothing ever matter? How could you sleep with him? How could you lay there next to him after making love, when I was alone 2 floors downstairs thinking how the hell to run away from this place? Did you ever loved me? Or you love him? You know what I think, that you always love him Cecillia. You don't know, but you love him, you cant live without him.

Shut up! You are disgusting.

You are Cecillia. I'm so sick of myself loving you. I love you. I love you with all of my heart. I was hoping that child to be mine, to be a girl beautiful as you, to love her like I loved you. Why Cecillia? Why did you do this to me? Why?

I loved you, but you need to understand if I leave all of it now, I lose my brother, I lose my child, I lose my money, my house, everything. For nothing?

Nothing? That is what you call me now? Nothing?

Darran, please go. You would never understand what is happening in my heart. I'm happy that I met you and I will never forget you. But my life is complicated and it will always be.

I hope your father is proud of you. I'm pretty sure that this is not what he wanted you to become.

Darran? Darran?

Cecillia? Let's go. It's time to pack everything. Bill told me to take you upstairs.

Why Tommy? Why?

Cecillia, listen you need to put yourself together for us. Come on. Let's go.

Bill, I'm so sorry for everything. I should new that you will never lie to me and take care of us. I'm so sorry...

It's ok love, don't worry. You did what every stupid young girl should do, I always knew that you come back to your senses. Come on let's go.

Guys, please can you take care of the rest of the house and furniture. If mister Bob comes to move, please tell him to contact me and I will explain why I have to leave.

Of course Sir, don't worry about nothing.

Come on Cecillia up you go. Come on Tommy you to.

The carriage start moving, leaving everything behind...

Cecillia?! Cecillia!!! Don't leave me, don't leave us. Please. Cecillia!!!

As the carriage was leaving the yard, Cecillia didn't have the power to look back and see Darran like this. She wanted to keep him in her mind like he was. A strong man who loved her with all his heart.

Cecillia don't do this, don't go. Cecillia...

Darran, it's over! Come on I will take you upstairs.

Leave me alone! Go away! You took her from me. And him. And everybody. All of you. Let me be...

The hours pass by, and as Cecillia was far far away from London, Darran was still there waiting for her. He couldn't imagine that all that they had for so many years, went by, like the wind.

Mate? It's over. I need to close the mansion, tomorrow the new owner is moving in. Nobody is coming back. You need to go.

Tommy, did you talk with your sister?

They are in the way to America, 2 more days I think with the ship. Cecillia is happy and safe.

How do you know that she is happy? She told you? Or Bill told you?

Doesn't matter how told me, she is better then here.

Well, I'm sure she is not. Because nobody asked her how she feels, if she is happy, if she needs something. It was only about you Tommy. You and him.

Me?

Yes, Tommy. You. Because if wasn't you, she could run away with me and be happy. She could be a woman, not a slave.

Listen Darran, I'm gone be honest with you. If Cecillia wanted to run away with you, I'm sure she would. You know why? Because if she left me with Bill, I don't think he will just throw me in the street. He care about me and he loved me. So I'm guessing that if she stayed with him for so many years, is because she wanted and maybe she loved him in her way. So be a man and get over it. It was a dream, a dream that you knew someday you gone wake up and it's over. I'm going...I hope you will find your true fate Darran, stay safe.

Bye Tommy. Send Cecillia my love when you see her.

I will. I promise.

Take care, kid.

Darran left from London back to his homeland. He knew that all of it wasn't a dream, it was love. The true meaning of love. He would never forget her, as she would never forget him.

In one early raining morning, he open the newspaper and the daily news was:

'Luxury Cruise Ship sank last night in the middle of the Atlantic Ocean'...
No survivors. A lot of important people lost their lives on the ship. Unfortunately no passengers survive the impact with the powerful storm.

The news stroke Darran's heart like an arrow. He would only imagine Cecillia's face when she was happy next to him, when they make love for hours and hours. He couldn't believe that the love of his life is dead. He couldn't breathe no more, his eyes were full of tears and his hands wrapped on the newspaper.

After all of this, apparently love is not the only thing in life that keeps us together.

www.ingramcontent.com/pod-product-compliance
Ingram Content Group UK Ltd.
Pitfield, Milton Keynes, MK11 3LW, UK
UKHW020424310726
14060UKWH00021B/25

9 780244 322397